Ellie and Her Emotional Dragons

Joseph Goodrich

Illustrated by Traci Van Wagoner

Published by Wisdom House Books, Inc.

Chapel Hill, North Carolina 27514 USA • 1.919.883.4669 • www.wisdomhousebooks.com

Wisdom House Books is committed to excellence
in the publishing industry.

Book design copyright © 2018 by Wisdom House Books, Inc.
All rights reserved.

Cover and Interior design by Krystal Smith • Cover and Interior Illustrations by Traci Van Wagoner (www.tracivanwagoner.com)

Published in the United States of America

Hardback ISBN: 978-1-73285530-4
LCCN: 2018961528

1. JUV039050   JUVENILE FICTION / Social Themes / Emotions & Feelings
2. JUV051000   JUVENILE FICTION / Imagination & Play
3. JUV002270   JUVENILE FICTION / Animals / Dragons, Unicorns & Mythical

First Edition

14 13 12 11 10 / 10 9 8 7 6 5 4 3 2 1

Ellie has four tiny dragons that magically
appear from her closet when she is

HAPPY,

SAD,

SCARED,

or

MAD.

NAZ

Naz is a green dragon that helps Ellie when she is nervous or scared.

NALI

Nali is a blue dragon that comforts Ellie when she is sad.

TULLY

Tully is a red dragon that calms Ellie when she is feeling mad.

Hani

And Hani is an orange dragon that loves to laugh and dance when Ellie is happy.

3

Ellie and her mommy and daddy just moved into an old house that makes strange noises that scare Ellie.

Creeaaak!

The radiator in the corner of her room makes a hissing sound, and the floor creaks when she walks near the bottom of her bed.

CLUNK!

CLANK!

CLINK!

ssssssso

hisssss

One day, Ellie jumped onto her bed and covered her head with her favorite blanket. Naz appeared from Ellie's closet.

"Ellie, why are you so scared?" Naz asked.

"This old house makes noises that scare me," Ellie said.

Naz looked over at the radiator making a hissing sound in the corner of Ellie's room.

"Ellie, it's okay to be scared of your new room. It takes time to get used to a new home."

Ellie took her head out from under the covers. "Sometimes the best thing to do when you are scared is to take a deep breath and tell the thing that scares you, 'I'm not scared of you anymore!'"

"Okay Naz, if you're not scared
then neither am I!" Ellie said excitedly.
Ellie walked over to the hissing radiator and said,
"I am not scared of you anymore!"

Naz was proud of Ellie for not being scared anymore, so he gave her a tiny dragon hug and disappeared into Ellie's closet.

Later that morning, Ellie's mom called.
"Ellie, come say goodbye to Daddy.
He's going to work."

Ellie ran out of her room towards her daddy, who was dressed in his pilot uniform. "I have to go to work now," Daddy said. "Be good for Mommy, and I'll be home soon."

10

Ellie felt
very sad and she
started to tear up.
She gave her daddy
a big hug.

"Daddy, please
don't go," she said.
"I will miss you."

"I'll be back before
you know it."

Ellie waved as
she watched
her daddy
drive away.

She ran to her room and began to cry.
Nali appeared from Ellie's closet.
"Why are you so sad, Ellie?" Nali asked.
"My daddy left, and I miss him." Ellie answered.

"It's okay to feel sad when your daddy goes to work;
it means you love him very much," Nali said.
"I like to draw pictures when I'm sad."

Ellie's
Art Supplies

Ellie looked up at Nali and wiped her eyes with her arm. Then she drew a picture of herself playing outside with her daddy.

"I'll give this to my daddy, and he can take it with him the next time he goes to work."

Nali was so proud of Ellie for not being
sad anymore, so she gave her a tiny dragon
hug and disappeared into Ellie's closet.

A few minutes later the doorbell rang.

DING! DONG!

"Hey, Ellie," Mom said. "Come meet our new neighbors, Jacob and his mommy." Ellie gave a little wave.
"Hello Jacob, I'm Ellie."
"Would you and Jacob like to go to your room and play?" mom said.
"Okay," Jacob said.
Jacob and Ellie ran to Ellie's room.

Jacob was looking around for something to play with when he found the picture Ellie drew for her daddy. He took the picture from Ellie's desk. "Who is this?"

Ellie's face turned red, and she started to get mad.

"Hey, that's not yours! Give it back!" she yelled. Ellie grabbed the picture to take it away from Jacob.

RRRiiiiiir!

It tore in half.

Jacob dropped his half and ran.

17

Before Ellie could chase after him, Tully appeared out
of her closet. "Ellie, why are you mad?" Tully asked.
"Jacob ripped my picture!" Ellie said.
"It was for my daddy and now it's ruined!"

"It's okay to feel mad when someone ruins something you worked hard to make," Tully said.

"But we can always draw another picture."

"Let's take three deep breaths together to calm down."

"In...Two...Three...Four...Out...Two...Three...Four..."

"In...Two...Three...Four...Out...Two...Three...Four..."

"In...Two...Three...Four...Ou'...Two...Three...Four..."

"There, now don't you feel better?"
Tully asked.
"Yup, I do," Ellie said calmly.
Now, I want to draw another picture for my daddy.

Tully was proud of Ellie for not being mad anymore, so he gave her a tiny dragon hug and disappeared into Ellie's closet.

Ellie was sitting at her desk to draw a new picture for her daddy when Jacob came back.

I brought tape.

"Ellie, I am sorry for ripping your drawing," Jacob said.

"I brought tape to fix it." Jacob taped both sides
of the picture together and handed it to Ellie.
"Thank you, thank you, thank you!"
Ellie said, jumping up and down.
"Now I can give it to my daddy when he gets home."

creeeaaak!

Later in the day, Ellie went into the kitchen to help Mommy cook dinner while they waited for Daddy to come home. The front door opened with a creak, but Ellie wasn't scared.

"Daddy's home!" Ellie shouted. She wasn't sad anymore.

She leaped into Daddy's arms and she handed him the neatly
taped picture, which she wasn't mad over anymore.
"I made this for you, and I made a new friend too."
"Super duper. This is the best picture ever," Daddy said.
"What's even better is playing soccer outside with my daughter."
"Just like in my drawing!" Ellie said.

"Yup," Daddy said. "Now, go get your ball."
Ellie wasn't scared, sad, or angry anymore. Instead, she was . . .

...HAPPY!

Ellie skipped to her room to get her soccer ball.

Hani appeared from her closet. "Why are you so happy?" Hani asked.

"I made a new friend, my daddy likes my drawing,

and we're going to play outside together!" Ellie said.

"When I'm happy I like to do my happy dance with a friend," Hani said.

Hani flew around Ellie's room while Ellie danced a happy dance too.

Hani was proud of Ellie for being happy,
so he gave her a tiny dragon hug and disappeared
back into Ellie's closet.

"Ellie, let's go play!" Daddy called.
Ellie played outside with her daddy before
eating dinner and getting ready for bed.

Ellie's mommy and daddy tucked her into bed
and kissed her good night.

As she began to fall asleep, Naz, Nali, Tully, and Hani flew out of Ellie's closet and snuggled next to her.

Good night, Nali. Thank you for helping me not be sad.

Good night, Tully. Thank you for helping me not be mad.